REVOLUTION

THE WHITE HORSE RIDER

VICTORIA BOYSON

REVOLUTION: THE WHITE HORSE RIDER
Copyright © 2016
All Rights Reserved.
Published by Kingdom House Press
ISBN:9780990608073

Victoria Boyson Ministries
www.victoriaboyson.com
victoria@boyson.org

REVOLUTION

THE WHITE HORSE RIDER

CONTENTS

For Cody Allen
& Cole Stephen

Our Father in heaven,
May Your name be kept holy.

May Your kingdom come soon.
May Your will be done on earth
as it is in heaven.

Matthew 6:9-10 NLT

INTRODUCTION

THE LORD IS as creative in communicating His truths to us as He is in designing His creation. I believe the visions and dreams He gives us are a lot like the parables He gave in the Bible, in which He teaches us His truths through stories. Many, including myself, learn His truth best from parables and visions.

This book is a series of visions the Lord has given me over several years. As He would call me to a visionary encounter with Him, it felt very much like being called to a visionary journey. I've tried to make it as descriptive as I saw it so you would feel as though you were right there with Beloved, our heroine.

I wanted to be faithful to the words He gave me and the imagery He showed me, so I could, without reservation, assure you it was from Him *to you.*

There is a war in the Church! The enemy has

been contending with the children of the kingdom from their beginning, yet his desperation is becoming more and more apparent. This enemy knows the kingdom of heaven is bursting onto the earth with a powerful and violent force.

Indeed, the Lord warned us of an impending forceful war between darkness and light. He said, *kingdom will rise against kingdom* (see Matthew 24:6), that is, the kingdom of light and the kingdom of darkness. The pressures we are feeling now are just the birth pangs of a great battle being fought for control of the spiritual atmosphere of earth and the realization of the next great awakening.

The Lord said, "I have come to set the world on fire, and I wish it were already burning!" (Luke 12:49 NLT) Our Lord did not come to bring peace to the world, but He came to wage a war for our hearts that would bring about a lasting peace, an eternal peace. Our Savior is determined to have His way in our planet, and He will.

For, although much of the battle is felt in the natural realm, our battle is not fought in the natural realm but in the supernatural realm. "We are human, but we don't wage war as humans do. We use God's mighty weapons, not worldly weapons, to knock down the strongholds of human reasoning and to destroy false arguments" (2 Corinthians 10:3-4).

For some time now, people in this world have reacted to the wins and losses of the supernatural war waged all around them. Indeed, abortion, murder, and perversion are merely the symptoms of this heavenly war we are in. Truly, this war is the war of the ages, a battle between the kingdoms of dark and light. Our battle is not as much about sin as it is the temperature of our love for our God—if we burn with red hot love for our Lord, sin isn't a pleasure to us.

To establish His kingdom on earth, we must first and most importantly establish His kingdom in our hearts. Our heart's cry must become His as we pray, "May your Kingdom come soon. May your will be done on earth, as it is in heaven" (Matthew 6:10). Our decree, our cry, our anthem for ourselves and for the body must become, "Let your kingdom come in my heart today!" Establishing His righteous rule in our lives, we radiate the government of heaven here on the earth overtaking the darkness with His powerful radiant light!

We all have the same goal: to advance the kingdom of God. If one of us succeeds, we all succeed; kingdom success belongs to the whole body. When we build up a brother or sister, we build up ourselves, for we are all the bride of Christ. When we are made as one—we are made stronger.

In Revelation 12:11 (NKJV), it says the bride of Christ "overcame him by the blood of the Lamb and by the word of their testimony, and they did not love their lives to the death." This is bible prophecy. It was not talking about the early church but about us!

This is truly the revelation of the bride of Christ—prophesying the beauty of Christ in us. While the rest of the world is busy loving themselves at the cost of all else, His bride will shine as we love. For love casts out fear, shines like a beacon, and liberates the captive—changing the world.

I

THE FATHER

LATE AT NIGHT upon the Lord's flattop mountain, Beloved lay among a gathering of faithful seekers where the prophetic host had come to rest in the Lord. Sleeping before a dimly lit fire, they were unaware of the invasion of a presence which permeated the mountain's stillness, seeming to alter the cold night's air.

Wrestling with her dreams, Beloved's sleep was suddenly taken captive by a powerfully invasive light, illuminating the night sky. Emerging from the center of an upended oval light stepped a knight dressed in brilliant armor from head to foot.

"Follow me," he whispered to her. As he motioned for her to come, he quickly moved ahead of her, urging her to follow him as he moved back toward the direction of the light.

"Quickly!" he said as he gestured for her to follow.

He moved swiftly toward the lighted portal, which seemed to be the entrance to another realm filled with intense, pure light. As the knight stepped quickly through the opening, he motioned for her to do the same.

Moving swiftly at first, Beloved followed him obediently, but suddenly hesitated. Frozen with awe, she felt motionless and unable to respond to his urging. The knight, however, seemed impatient for her to move and turned away from her to step back through the opening.

Questioning the risk, hesitation flooded her heart. She knew she wanted very much to accompany him, but everything was happening so quickly. As her emotions took over her heart, the portal started to close as he stepped through it.

Startled by his sudden departure, Beloved cried out, "NO! Don't leave me!" She knew she had to move at once, so bravely ran after him, entering just before it closed behind her.

Inside, she was blinded by the purest white light—light she felt possessed a fiery, powerful presence, which seemed to penetrate her soul. Adjusting her eyes to the light, Beloved stood motionless, not knowing quite what to do. Watching the knight approach a glorious white throne that seemed to fill the radiant room, she sheepishly did the same.

It was the throne of God.

Beloved stared at the powerfully wonderful Being sitting atop the great royal throne. Light emanated from Him and filled the whole room. Next to Beloved, the knight fell to one knee. Feeling as though she was being led by the knight, she hurried to do the same.

She could not help but stare at the Great One on the throne. He returned her gaze, expressing the purest most tender love. His face, so full of light, was suddenly illuminated by a powerful explosion of white fire, sending out a tremendous glory-filled mushroom cloud around Him.

Twice, the glorious cloud covered Him, filling the area around His throne as His resplendence unfurled about Him in all directions, pulsating with intense power and then it was suddenly drawn back into Himself.

He called for Beloved to come closer to Himself. Motioning for her to sit at His feet, He was overjoyed at having her there, His delight filled the room with energy and glorious light. Truly, He was her heavenly Father.

Other than the knight, the Father appeared to be alone and yet, as she watched Him, ethereal beings seemed to ebb and flow in and out of Him. His Presence appeared to reach outside Himself in long lines of electrified energy that were to her like arms that filled the room with streams of luminance.

The extending arms of lights were as weightless and airy as feathers and Beloved wondered if they, themselves, were a mysterious kind of Elysian creature she hadn't yet encountered. As her thoughts were caught in a drift of amazement, she suddenly realized *He* was addressing her.

His great hands were now full of feathers as bright white and powerful as He was. Handing the feathers to her, she understood they were to be her reward for the pain and persecution she had endured through her many battles for the destiny of the inhabitants of the earth.

"Do you remember what I promised you, Beloved?"

He'd promised her so many things, she marveled

at His question.

"Remember, Beloved?" He asked patiently. "I promised you wings, dear one."

Raising His arms full of feathers, He motioned to her, "For you, Beloved. Your feathers... Yours, precious, you have earned them." He smiled patiently while she gathered her stunned thoughts.

Suddenly, as He spoke, she saw it all in her spirit. She could see that every time she had been the target of attack by humans or demons, she was also made the target of God's grace and His strategic mercy. And as she was faithful to forgive and stay in His love when she was reviled, the Father, too, was building up a heavenly account of His grace and mercy, keeping it in waiting for her. Indeed, mercy was His way of giving her the wings He had promised her many years previously.

He motioned for her to come even nearer to Him.

Moving closer, He showed her the robe He wore. It was covered in the identical feathers He had just given her. Intending that Beloved should see a section of His robe which had been robbed of its feathers, she soon realized He had taken *her* feathers from His *own garment*.

Shocked by the realization, her hand rushed to

9

cover her open mouth as she let out a startled cry, "NO, Papa! Father, no! Don't ruin your beautiful robe for me!" she pleaded with Him.

However, it was His own great pleasure that she should know what He had done for her. *"You will always have a piece of Me with you, Beloved—a portion of My strength and covering. You will understand your sacrifice has been dearly rewarded and it will increase your faith when you need it most."* He nodded His head lovingly, wanting her to receive what He was telling her.

Shocked by His sacrifice, it humbled her to accept this costly gift from Him. But she understood the gift's power and the impact it would have on her life's quest.

Allowing her a moment to accept His gift, He then motioned to the top of her head as a golden crown suddenly appeared. Across the tremendous crown read the word, "VICTORIOUS," gleaming with the light from the fire of His face shining against it.

"It will open doors for you, Beloved." He beamed with delight as He told her.

Suddenly, she was made aware of an intriguing golden necklace that suddenly appeared around her neck reading, "SALVATION." Marveling at it, she watched in awe as the word salvation cried a single tear, and in the shape of a heart, one teardrop of blood fell from the necklace, landing carefully and purposefully in the palm of Beloved's hand.

"This is My love," He spoke with great tenderness. "When they see it, they will know and feel My love for them. I've shown My love for them through My Son's blood, the blood of a great Warrior King. He's fought for them and I have given Him many souls because of it. And in return, He's given them back to Me."

"Share My love, Beloved, and I will give you souls as well."

Beloved struggled under the weight of all she was experiencing and still He continued to reveal even more treasures He held for her. Reaching beside Him, He caught up a handful of golden arrows and placed them in her lap.

"You will need these too, dear. They will increase your authority in prayer—they are powerful in battle."

A sword, very large and heavy, was the next gift He presented her. "This sword will help you to stand strong as the winds of deception are launched against you; it will make you a shelter of protection for your comrades and it has immense power to annihilate your enemies. Keep your sword close to you at all times, for it also has the power to refresh your heart when you need it most. I've given you a large sword, because I know how much you love to share with others."

Heaving a sigh and grabbing her hand in His, the Father drew His well-loved child very close to Him. As He placed her head tenderly on His knee, she began to cry. She was simply overwhelmed by His tender love and thoughtful tribute, but He was not finished.

He drew her face even closer toward His, and His eyes seemed to glow with wonder. "Look at my face, Beloved." He smiled at her with bright eyes, clear with the purity of love so indescribable it took her breath away.

Sparkling with absolute glee, His face displayed the obvious emotions of an adoring Father's affection for His dear child. He wanted her to see it. He wanted her to experience Him as He truly was.

Almost overwhelming her, He peered into Beloved's face for what seemed to her a remarkably long time. He wanted her to learn Him, experiencing the brightness of His countenance and the extreme joy of His smile. White hair and white beard, His face was framed by love—the joyous, delightful affection of a dear, sweet Father's unbridled passion for His child.

His love penetrated her soul...

Consuming every hidden remnant of her heart, she felt His love wash through her like the waves of a mighty ocean. Overpowered by His love for her, she felt wave after wave of His powerful acceptance wash through her soul. As it did, the truest love imaginable changed years of rejection into an impassioned adoption by Him.

Beloved felt, with great certainty, nothing that had happened to her in the past would ever again hold any power over her. As the past washed away in His gaze, all insecurity, inadequacy, rejection and self-doubt vanished in His eyes.

Filled with His love, she felt His words pulsating through her mind, "Tell them you've seen My face, Beloved. Tell them... It's My desire that My children pursue My face. I will not hide from those who seek Me with their whole heart. I long for them to see Me as I am!"

Her Father smiled at her one last time before the knight who'd led her to Him rose to stand by her side, and she felt compelled to follow his lead. Her soul wanted to stay with Him; the memory of His face would stay with her forever.

13

She thought, "Who will believe me? Who will believe *I* have seen *Him* in this way?" Beloved felt His purpose and His design, His need and delight, that she should see Him this way.

"Nothing will ever take it away from me. It is mine forever!" Beloved declared.

᷈

Suddenly shaken by the recollection of the presence of the valorous knight by her side, she turned toward him.

Beloved looked at him as if for the first time – he was amazingly elegant, and so powerfully serene. Her mind was now flooded with questions about this beautiful knight who refused to leave her side.

"Wait..." she tried to force herself to embrace the moment she was experiencing.

"Wait..." she wondered again, stalling until she could think through their recently shared experience.

She was beginning to realize who he was. She smiled as her heart rose with expectancy. Filled with joy over her sudden realization, she answered her own question. Stumbling over her words, she smiled broadly, "Of course you are, yes, you are, my Jesus.

My Knight! *My own Beloved!"*

She rested in His arms and sighed in His protective comfort.

2

THE LORD'S DELIGHT

JOYOUSLY ECSTATIC OVER the sudden realization of who her Guide actually was, Beloved was awestruck as she looked at Jesus.

Powerful and elegant as He walked with her, He casually reached around her and covered her shoulders with a luxuriously heavy, regal robe designed to bring her comfort. She had turned to watch Him and saw, amazingly, the robe He'd given her was beautifully embroidered with a large gold cross displayed boldly on the back.

"What royalty!" she exclaimed to Him.

"Truly," He said, stifling a snicker. "In My Father's house are many... *robes...*" He chuckled. He sought to ease the intensity of her heart after the overwhelming encounter she had just experienced with the Father. "Would you like to see more of heaven?" He asked her.

Overjoyed by what He offered, she replied with an effervescent, "Yes!"

"What would you like to see, Beloved?"

Caught off guard by His question, she didn't know how to answer. As she hesitated, a thought sprang to her mind. "What place would *You* like to show me?"

Jesus smiled that strong broad smile of His and reached over and grabbed her hand. He seemed delighted, almost mischievous, as He led her to a little white building that resembled a simple cafe. Walking through the door, Beloved looked around and saw booths and a few customers filling the relatively small room.

She looked up to the Lord with a face filled with inquiry as He responded with a laugh, and a, "Just wait." He motioned with His hands to the order counter of the cafe.

Beloved watched in amazement as a small child walked up to the counter and then quickly walked back from where he'd come from, only to return again bringing several other children with him.

Hurrying to follow their friend, a crowd of four to five children quickly made their way to the counter to greet, it would seem, one of their favorite and most familiar customers. Their friend and playmate, Jesus, had come in to the restaurant to play with them, and they were delighted.

Jesus introduced Beloved to His playmates, and they were happy to meet her, but were all business as they *played* restaurant. Moving swiftly into their familiar positions, they stood at attention as the Lord looked over the menu. Anticipating His order, they all stood bright-eyed with captive delight.

Easily stepping into His role as the customer, Jesus hid His smile and very seriously ordered a meal for them to prepare. As He proceeded through the ordering, each child would jump to attention and rush to begin their preparations for serving the Lord. With the greatest seriousness, they worked energetically to cook for and serve the King of kings. And He enjoyed every minute as equal attention was given to Beloved's order as well.

When orders were taken care of in a professional

manner, they assured them both of their quick fulfillment. As Jesus and Beloved left the counter, they took a seat at a nearby booth.

Watching the activity in the kitchen, Beloved took the opportunity to probe Him about the restaurant. Charmed by her delight, He beamed as He shared the details of one of His favorite spots in heaven.

"This place is famous! People love to visit the children as they *play* restaurant; it truly is a real *pretend* cafe that only kids are allowed to work at. All of heaven cherishes it. They love to patronize it, not for the food necessarily, but for the atmosphere of play, which the kids, of course, take *very* seriously," He laughed.

After what seemed like such a short time, a crowd of activity came pouring out of the kitchen into the dining area. A small dutch door connected to the order counter flew open, pushed by a youthful, giggling gang of pretend waiters and cooks. The children approached their booth.

Fighting back signs of pleasure, they each very professionally delivered cups, plates, and baskets brimming with their concoctions. With sincere delight, they watched as Jesus responded to their anticipation with a large, hearty bite of a very cheesy macaroni dish they'd prepared for Him.

"Ahhhhh..." came His exaggeratedly scrumptious response. The children filled the room with sounds of joyous satisfaction as they twirled in delight with playful "relief." Grown-up customers from all corners of the room joined the group in their occasion for fun!

Beloved felt she could have stayed in that place forever. She was elated to have been so privileged to watch her Lord at play. He didn't seem at all to be placating the children, but was genuinely enjoying His time with them and was artful in His role as patron.

She started to think more about Him. She thought she knew what He was like, but there was so much more depth to Him than she'd ever wondered about previously.

Her curiosity grew as she watched Him, when suddenly He turned to her quite unexpectedly.

"Beloved, dear, how about a go around the place?" He said, feeling quite relaxed after His time with the children.

Caught off guard, Beloved was drawn out of her thoughts, "A *go,* Lord?" she asked. But her question came too late. He wasn't waiting for a response, He was having too much fun. He whisked her arm in

His and, saying, "Bye," to the children, He headed out the door.

Her marvel increasing, Beloved was completely captivated by Jesus. Her curiosity delighted Him. Completely free from any of the plaguing fears and insecurities of earth, she trusted the Lord absolutely and wanted to prolong their time together.

With her arm in His, they were both suddenly caught up in the Spirit atop a large breathtakingly beautiful hill in heaven. From its vantage point they could see all the extraordinary views of His home. His broad smile filled His face and His eyes lit up as He pointed out to her His favorite landscape and preferred hills.

Laughing, the Lord suddenly transported them both to the base of a beautiful ravine He cherished. But she didn't understand why He was laughing. Jesus was giddy with excitement to reveal a surprise He had in store for her.

Rounding the corner of the ravine, and pointing at what appeared to be a brand new Model-A Ford, a broad smile filled His lovely face. "Look at that!" He said bursting into laughter again.

Beloved was astonished!

A stunningly beautiful convertible in burgundy-red with leather seats and wooden accents showed off as if it were brand new and just rolled off the assembly line the day before.

Full of questions, Beloved squealed with delight, "You have cars in heaven? How? Why do you have cars in heaven?"

Anticipating her inquisition, He grinned and shot back, "We just like them!"

Beloved screamed with joy, "Take me for a ride!"

Anticipating a heavenly drive through the hills, she was shocked when the car lifted into the air and *flew.* The Lord gently glided His car through the sky, passing over the hills and valleys they'd just walked through. As they continued, they passed over lovely, heavenly saints. In her excitement, Beloved waved down at them and they, in turn, waved and hollered out, *"Hello, Beloved,"* as if they'd always known her.

After they'd flown awhile, Jesus told Beloved to look in the back seat of the car. Turning around to see what His next surprise for her was, she found a pile of opulent pearls, each about an inch in diameter. Extraordinarily luminous, she gathered up the biggest handful she could muster and just held them in her hands.

She squealed with enthusiasm as each pearl seemed to reflect a whole world of creativity back at her.

The Lord freely said, "You can have as many as you like!"

Again, He told her to look in the back seat. She whirled about, anticipating another grand surprise. But when she looked this time, she saw the sweetest little kitten, ever-so darling, mostly black with perfect little white feet.

"Awww, how precious! What do you call him?"

"Socks."

Beloved drew the precious bundle up and snuggled her face in his and, feeling no fear whatsoever, she asked confidently, "Oh, how sweet. Can I have it?"

The Lord laughed and answered, "Well...you can hold him."

Holding the little fella, Beloved thought about how He'd placed greater value on the kitten than He had the pearls. He'd eagerly told her to take all she wanted of the pearls, and yet when she asked about the kitten, He didn't want to relinquish His little Socks to her.

Having a greater understanding of Him now, this newest revelation of His character made her love Him even more. Things, even so-called *great treasure,* mattered very little to Him, and yet people and animals were what He value most.

The happy pair flew over several more best-loved canyons and hills, seeking out all the Lord's favorite places for adventure.

Looking over the endless landscape of heaven and knowing there was so much more to see than what she'd been shown, she thought to herself, *"It would be impossible to ever be bored up here."*

Looking down at picturesque ravines and valleys, she watched as the peaceful people of heaven enjoyed the countryside of paradise. Again, everyone she caught sight of gave her a hearty wave and greeted her as if they knew her personally and loved her. Their greetings flooded her heart with overwhelming acceptance—a very powerful acceptance that seemed to penetrate her spirit and affect her physical body.

Over the breathtaking oceans she stared with great interest at the people enjoying the water, as if on holiday, on what seemed to her to be every type of boat ever made, and some she did not recognize. Historical vessels sailed alongside present-day boats and yet, to her, they all appeared brand new.

Beloved noticed the Lord had grown quiet, and she turned toward Him as if He needed her. His expression changed and His countenance became much more serious. "What is it, Lord?" Beloved asked. "What's troubling you?"

He did not answer her, but instead landed His beautiful car gently on the green lawn overlooking the crystal-blue sea nearby.

Turning to face her, He spoke, "Beloved, you were not brought here to see these things... but you were called to witness something of great magnitude that will affect pronounced change on the earth. You've been summoned to observe the preparations heaven is making to advance their charge into the spirit-realms of earth. Are you willing to witness it?"

Feeling her heart grow steadily more concentrated with the weight of the intensity the Lord carried in His, she recognized the feeling of steadfast urgency He held for the earth's imperative need.

"Yes, Lord," was all she could answer and then, suddenly, He was gone.

3

Heaven's Army

ALONE NOW, Beloved was immediately surrounded by the angelic sweeping in around her from all sides, appearing to her like a glorious light-filled cloud. She was transported by them and conveyed to another place in heaven entirely.

It was the aroma of this new place that caught her attention at first. As the cloud around her dissipated, she saw only the faint outline of a tremendous army. What she saw at last took her breath away.

Covering the hillsides of heaven stood a breathtaking army literally brimming with rushed activity. Cloaked by a mysterious fog, Beloved was only able to view their actions through brief glimpses.

She could make out a mighty army moving efficiently, readying itself for an impending battle. Beloved saw flashes of running feet and chariot wheels partnered with labored breathing and rapid succession of angelic warriors preparing themselves for battle. As these ethereal warriors clad themselves in radiant, silver armor, an amber glow rose from the base of the army, aiding the intensely clouded sky hovering over them.

Beloved listened as the sky reverberated with the anxious sounds of grunting and unintelligible chatter while they fitted out horses for their heavenly riders. As she watched in eager wonder, intense, mighty Elysian beings readied their massive beasts.

The long, high-pitched neighing of horses and their nervous whinnies filled the weighty atmosphere around the awaiting army. Inarticulate grunting could be heard as riders struggled to master the overanxious movements of the imperial beasts resisting their caretakers. Moving their powerful heads in sharp angled movements, they reared back on their immense legs with great strength, their breath shooting up into the lucid, ethereal sky.

Accompanied by extraordinary creatures of heavenly origin unknown to the earth, and the angelic who serve the sons of man, the warriors worked as one vast confident machine. Storehouses full of unearthly artillery crafted for the annihilation of those forces who'd taken captive the minds of man were emptied to equip the large army. Heavenly weapons were swiftly taken up and conveyed to each warrior of the Light.

Magnificent banners were ceremoniously unfurled with confident urgency. Filling the army with affectionate satisfaction in the grandiosity of their strength and glory, the celebrated banners were alive with the tangible powers of the empyrean realm. Their power could be seen sweeping through the army having a noticeable impact on their splendor.

Anticipating the urgency of their entry into earth's kingdoms, the firmament was brimming with impatient expectation. Heaven had been vigilantly waiting for this hour since the beginning of time.

As the fog began to lift, Beloved could now see across the expanse of heaven and beheld a truly magnificent array of the most extraordinary warriors she'd ever seen. Indeed, it was an army of Divine light. Horse and rider were ready and marching at attention. Moving together as one force, the preparedness of this army shifted the weight of the atmosphere in the universe and the earth felt the consequences of its presence.

Flying high above the radius of the great army below, a lone rider sat atop an enormous, gleaming white horse. With wings that filled the expansive sky, the great horse conveyed a warrior of golden fire more brilliant than the steed on which He rode. The strikingly regal display of immeasurable power made her heart stagger in response.

Frozen by His breathtaking magnificence, she was captivated by His appearance. His face was framed by hair that seemed to flow as fire behind Him like the mane of a great lion. Streaming out all around Him and covering His brilliant armor, the Rider's robe was alive. Cascading down the back of the brilliant beast He rode, the robe flowed like liquid fire tipped in blood. His golden-brown hair was wild, streaked with the rays of the glorious light that shown out from His face.

Like a mighty wave in an ocean tempest, Beloved watched as a cloud of fire roared all around Him and His massive steed. Rolling in all directions inside of itself, it filled the realm of the Divine as He rode.

Building in violent intensity, the storm labored to birth a massive celestial nimbus nebula. Crowning Him in light, it framed Him in a halation aureole, transcending the regions of heaven. Stunned, yet without fear, Beloved felt certain she could see human faces appearing occasionally in the cloud as it rotated violently.

Assembling into harmonious echoes, she heard an alarming roar from the depths of heaven as all the believers in heaven travailed in unison for the extraordinary army. The army instantly responded as an all-encompassing, penetrating, bright light *burst* forth from the Rider. Beloved was jolted by its intensity.

Realizing she was surrounded by the expectant bride of heaven, she was astounded by the vehement intensity of the saints who'd joined her. Together, they created a realm of fiery passion, which gripped the army.

Building to a fever pitch, the increased expectancy in the atmosphere grew to an almost violent level toward an enemy who sought to thwart their well-loved Father's worship on earth.

Heaven had been anxiously awaiting this day: the saints, angels and all the amazing creatures of heaven had anticipated His call. It seemed their hearts would burst with the love and pride they'd held for the children of the earth who were so terribly desperate for His help. How they had been longing for the Father's promised help. He would, indeed, invade the earth and fight the armies of darkness, which pervaded the realms surrounding it.

Instinctively, Beloved knew it would be a ferocious battle. She trembled when she realized what the earth must endure as the Light of heaven overwhelmed the darkness oppressing it.

Nearly suffocating from the darkness attempting to take possession of the realms of the earth, heaven's earthly loved ones desperately needed the Father to manifest Himself for their sake as well as for the lost kingdom heirs.

Truly, the collected prayers of the intercessors, harvested for centuries, would be carried into battle for, a great multitude of the angelic carried enormous golden bowls of intercession—the prayers of the ages. Indeed, this would be a battle they would fight *together*—a universal war of the armies of the Light together with His bride taking on the armies of darkness.

Prophesies from both heaven and earth combined to create a vernacular storm of vengeance upon their enemy. Every prophecy of the Presence ever uttered would be carried into this battle and each would bring a necessary victory to earth.

All at once, she felt a powerful force break upon her, nearly knocking her over. Beloved's body jerked back as if from the power of a tremendous blast. She whirled around with explosive excitement, and gasped, "What, Lord!?"

Catching herself, she scrambled to see what was happening. Her body seemed paralyzed as she realized all around her, indeed, the entire bride in heaven suddenly erupted with a mighty roar!

"Gooooooooooo!" they screamed toward His bride on earth.

She could feel the breath of the saints as they screamed all around her. "Gooooooooooo!"

"Gooooooooooo!" they screamed at the earth again and again.

Beloved could also hear individual heartfelt cries. "Go! I wish I could be with you!" she heard them cry to their loved ones on earth as they wept for joy at the impending victory that was a certainty.

"Our prayers are with you!" another unanimous roar lifted from the massive crowd in rapturous joy.

"Finally, we are *one bride*," Beloved thought to herself. "His bride will be one with Him at last." Heaven and earth would, indeed, join forces in heart and mind as they were finally made one in Him.

"Ruuuuuuuunnnn!" they roared again in increasing strength. As their excitement rose, they screamed together at the earth with a massive, powerful force that seemed to penetrate it and shake its mighty mountain ranges.

Truly, the prayers of all the saints from heaven and earth combined to create a massive roar that filled the heavenlies, released to powerfully impact the earth! Light filled the sky around them as the angels brandished their swords. Reflecting the light of the Father, they called to the saints.

Again, like thunder that shook heaven, the angels roared to the saints, "Nooooooooowwww!"

Beloved did not know where to look. Her heart beat with fevered anticipation.

"What would happen next?" she wondered.

The saints knew this was the moment they had been anticipating for thousands of years. All of heaven knew full well what those on the earth would endure. But they were not afraid. No. This would be the earth's greatest hour!

As if invaded by an unseen force, Beloved felt the glory of God rise within her and fill the whole of His heavenly bride. It seemed as though they had all been caught by His invisible hand, and their merging energies were suddenly captivated, blending together into a massively powerful force filled with purposeful expectation.

"But, what were they waiting for?" she wondered to herself impatiently.

Then, with a great shout, they began to praise. As they did, they called to the Father to release the Lamb of God. With one voice, led by one Spirit and filled with the passionate love of their Father, together they called forth to the earth *the White Horse Rider!*

With the echoes of the call to the White Horse Rider still resounding through her like the force of a trumpet, Beloved realized she was no longer in heaven. She felt now only the last remaining echoes of their calling filling the air of, what was on earth, a very quiet night.

All around her on the mountain's crown lay the host just as she had left them.

Resetting to earth's realm again, Beloved gasped violently for breath!

Stunned by the scene she'd just witnessed,

Beloved cried out, "PAPA! Don't leave me. Please Father!"

Wanting nothing more than to have the assurance He was still with her, to comfort her and love her like only a Divine Father can, she cried for Him again. "Papa!" Breaking down, she wept until morning began to break.

4

HEAVEN TO EARTH

AS MORNING BROKE over the mountain, all Beloved could do was pray. She prayed to know the Father to greater degrees; she was completely captivated by Him and yearned to know *everything* about Him. She tried desperately to ingest all she'd seen and experienced in heaven. She surrendered to her hunger for Him, realizing there was so much more of Him and so many more aspects of His personality she'd not yet learnt.

Legendary in the universe, she was overwhelmed by Him, both by His power and the depth of His love. He was truly Almighty, yet He wanted her. Beloved marveled at the layers of His complex simplicity.

Understanding how suddenly ill-fitted she felt for earth, the faithful angelic had prepared for her a beautifully burnished bowl. Laden with a bounty of heaven's liquid glory, the celestial servants were overjoyed to present it to Beloved as a preparation for the destiny that lay before her.

She readily received heaven's precious offering and happily lifted it above her head and poured it generously over herself. Absorbing the tranquil amity of the Father's heavenly home, it covered her as the flame seeped deep inside her.

Bathed by His golden glory, she felt its luminous, molten fire go deep inside her spirit, filling the innermost parts of her soul.

In awe and anticipation, she anxiously waited for what was to happen next.

It was then Beloved felt a prayer burst forth from her spirit. With intense emotion she cried out, "Father, let Your kingdom come in me; let Your will be done in me. Father, let the reality of Your kingdom be established in me."

Captivated by the presence of eternity, she then turned to the prophetic host and again back to Him and prayed fervently, "Father, let Your will be done in Your host!"

❧

Morning passed quickly and as the host rested around the dying embers of the night's fire, the morning light penetrated the dimmed sky and they were waking to the full warmth of the morning sun's light.

Beloved was surrounded by her fellow warriors, the prophetic host and seekers who pursued Him. In them, she'd found the family she'd always yearned for. They enjoyed together the victories and blessings their Father bestowed on them. Sharing their joy, they saw it multiply, filling each other with the eternal power of heavenly blessings.

As Beloved continued her communion with the Father, she was oblivious to their rising. They had felt the gentle Spirit pervading their campsite atop the quiet mountain and delighted in the presence of the precious Guide they all knew well. Waiting patiently while Beloved shared discourse with the

Lord, they could not help but join her in adulation.

In a tender display of their shared communion, they knelt in the morning air and shared the feast the Father had prepared for them. From the table of His heart, He fed them, first His empowering encouragement, and then His wisdom and strength, and each shared in His joy.

From heaven to earth, the host reveled in the choicest heavenly provisions for their day's journey as the angelic delivered heaven's commissariat and spiritual nourishment to the militant tribe. All around them the angelic expressed their overwhelming pleasure of the Father's heart toward His cherished warriors.

As their worship increased in response to the blessing of His presence, He increased Himself even more. And together they filled the mountain's atmosphere with a celebration of shared love and appreciation.

The joy expressed by the Father and His warriors overflowed onto the angels who were simply captivated by the shared joy they saw displayed. They couldn't help but to rejoice and dance in the irresistible pleasure they felt.

The angelic danced in the worship of the seekers, doing somersaults in the streams of glory descending from the Father that filled the sky like trails of free-flying glory dust. Laughing out loud, they felt giddy in the streaming resplendency as His joy reached from heaven filling each seeker as they worshiped.

As they shared the feast of the Lord, their discussion grew much more serious when Beloved spoke of the hour that was soon approaching the earth. It was disconcerting to them, for none of them relished the idea of war. Yet, it was war they were entering, a time of unprecedented supernatural war, between the kingdom of Light and the kingdom of darkness.

With ardent prayer they'd anticipated this day, but knew it would not be easy. Truly, the kingdom of their Father was at war with the dark powers of the earth and they'd anticipated the opportunity to pull down the evil strongholds that had plagued the earth for centuries.

It was their Father's enemy who had attempted to rule over mankind in an effort to thwart the worship of God's children and suck the life from His creation. Though he had thrown the entire weight of his dark powers at them, he had failed to stop the expansion of the King of kings—Jesus. And now, the King of heaven was once again expected to enter the supernatural realms of earth to war against His adversary and buckle the gates of this world, establishing the government of His kingdom on earth in His children.

As the host were encouraged, Beloved shared with them the heightening of the supernatural war and the preparations of the army in heaven. They felt moved by the calling of the Lord as He established His watchmen to awaken His bride.

"As He is glorified in us," they prayed together, "let the Light of His kingdom dawn on the earth and be established *in it as it is in heaven.*"

And, "His bride will be awakened and transformed!" became their unified declaration. "For His glory," they continued, "He will transform His church into the most breathtaking, captivating bride ever imagined. This glorious, beautiful bride will rise and rule in His love and the world for a time will be transformed."

Excited and emboldened by the advancement of His kingdom, the host began to discuss amongst themselves their plans for their victory over the darkness. "We must plan our next move, friends..."

Beloved felt anxious, for their focus seemed to subtly shift from submission to the Father to an emphasis of reliance on self-power. And in their excitement for their anticipated victory, they talked less of His power and leading.

She felt she had to speak up. "Gentle friends, may I remind you of the failures of earth's ancestors. Who, indeed, won when they obeyed the Father, but failed when they took matters into their own hands. It is only in His leading power that victory will come to us. No matter what the oracles counsel, we cannot execute His design *without Him.*"

"Remember, it is His will *from heaven to earth* and *not earth to heaven.* Our victory is in our continued journey *with Him.*" Her heart brimmed with her love and concern for them.

"Very nice, dear Beloved," they said with little regard for the weightiness of her words. They were lost in the honor of their seemingly imminent victory, and her voice carried much less weight than it seemed to on previous occasions.

Beloved's wise counsel was lost to them and she was overwrought with anxiety for the future of her friends. Moreover, she was frustrated that her wisdom had been so easily cast aside.

She was much more hurt than confused by their

ambivalence, and was dismayed by how little regard they'd had for the wisdom the Lord gave her. With eyes cast down, she fought hard to gain understanding, when something captured her attention.

It was the angelic motioning to her, calling her. Instantly, she understood what she needed to do, and she left the host to be alone.

Seeking solitude, she wandered to her favored place, a fissure fixed on the backside of the mountain range. She thirsted for His peace again and sought His wisdom for herself. Finding refuge, she threw herself against the rocky ledge and fell to her knees.

Looking up to her Father and heaven, she remembered His face. "Father?" she cried.

Suddenly, a beaming, bright light broke through all around—He had been expecting her!

Beloved disappeared.

❧

Brought together by a common love, the prophetic host was much more like family than their actual earthly families. As seekers, they had become a supernatural team with incredible love and true friendship. Awakened for His purpose, they were never apart in Spirit and leaned on each other tremendously.

Though they had, indeed, faced fierce battles and endured painful trials, they were, at times, still limited by their incomplete view of themselves. Not understanding the strength of their humility and the grace it possessed, they leant their ears to fear's augmented reasoning and were convinced they would not be enough on their own.

Unfortunately, instead of answering His leading with instant obedience, they argued with the leading of the Lord. Manipulated by fear's lies, they decided to pursue the help of warriors whom they considered to be more powerful than themselves.

Thusly, remaining through the night in disciplined excitement, the host reasoned amongst themselves how best to plan for the impending battle that faced them. In their fervor, they were, however, carried away by *their* plans. Refusing to heed Beloved's words, they continued to plan as they had been.

Deciding amongst themselves who they agreed would be the best warriors to evoke for battle, they questioned, "Who will convey the most influence? Who will bring the most support? Who will draw the most people?"

Unfortunately, not one of them thought to ask the most imperative question, "Who will bring the favor of the Lord?"

And so, they continued through the day in giddy anticipation for what they'd assumed would be their greatest victory yet...

5

The Children of His Presence

CAUGHT UP BY the Spirit, Beloved found herself transported to the site of an old, abandoned school edifice. She was quite stunned by the condition of the old school she had once cherished, which had been destroyed by the many earthquakes that had shaken the earth as the realms of heaven drew nearer.

All the old, beautiful buildings she treasured were now only rubble, piled in heaps of rotted wood and brick. She wanted to explore what had been the grounds of the formerly much loved school to see if there were parts yet left intact. But as she wandered through it, she grew to be quite distressed by its repellent state.

Overwhelmed by the sadness she felt over the condition of the campus, Beloved rambled aimlessly. Yet, led by the inner witness of her heart, she ventured through the remains of the buildings, which had at one time been her world. Nothing had been left untouched by the quaking effect of heaven's advancing presence.

All that was crippled or weakened by mankind's self-made foundations lain through the fleshly nature of man could not stand as the Lord's power affected it. It collapsed, crumbling like kingdoms made of sand.

Beloved was saddened, but she sensed all had not been completely destroyed. *"No,"* she thought to herself. *"It cannot all be gone. I can feel the presence of the Comforter leading me here."* She felt confident her well-loved Guide who'd loved her and comforted her all her life had led her to this place, but for what reason?

Would He reveal Himself to her here in this desolate place? She could only hope.

Room by room, building by building, Beloved

searched desperately. Just as she had begun to doubt the voice of her Guide, she felt Him lead her to the old chapel, which had, in the past, been a cherished place for her—a place where she had encountered the Father and been so changed by Him. Searching in earnest for the door of the beautiful old chapel, hope rose in her heart.

She found it already swung wide open, barely attached to its hinges and frame. As she climbed, a pile of debris attempted to subvert her entrance. Finally, wrestling through the barriers in front of it, she was met with lonely darkness. Cold, damp and dark, the old chapel seemed as empty as every other building she'd entered.

And yet... she listened intently, she stood quietly in the pitch-black foyer of what had been the chapel. She was almost certain she had heard something. Waiting to hear it once again, she abruptly whirled around to catch sight of what had originated the sound she'd heard behind her.

Curious to discover the source of the noise, she stood stunned, surprised to find a small child. A little boy of about seven years old stood watching her smartly as if he had been expecting her.

Fearlessly, the little whelp directed a big broad smile at Beloved. As his eyes sparkled with charmed impudence, she was instantly taken in by him.

"Hello, Beloved," he beamed as he greeted her as if he were an adult.

Returning his cheerful greeting, she smiled as he reached out his hand to clutch hers. "My name is Peter."

Shocked by his familiarity with her, she was too taken aback by him to reply. Taking his hand, she allowed him to lead her, but was too amazed by the little man to think much about where she was going.

It didn't take long for him to find a passage through the maze of rubble, which led to what remained of the chapel. Under half-broken beams and fallen ceilings, she followed him as he worked his way into the ruins.

Around what was left of an inside wall, she followed her new friend until at last they arrived at what was left of the inner workings of the sanctuary. Upon only a few remaining unmarred pews sat a marvelous display of children.

"Who has been using this old place?" Beloved turned questioningly toward Peter, but he was gone. Before she could resolve her questions, Beloved was soon struck by an intense Presence that held a great light.

Stupefied by the presence of her Holy Guide

dwelling in such a dilapidated old place, she stood expressionless until her eyes began adjusting to what she was seeing.

Holy Spirit had led her here, and what a treasure He'd led her to. Far greater than any glory that had previously occupied the old chapel, it was now a most treasured dwelling for the Great Presence.

Indeed, in the Spirit, this cherished sanctuary had not been destroyed or laid bare. But, truly, was made far more beautiful by His presence residing here than it had been, and was far more treasured by heaven than in its former days. Thought by men to be desolate and left in neglect, it had now become a most honored dwelling of the Creator. He'd chosen to treasure and dwell in it due to the captivating faith of the children who made it theirs.

Beloved was enthralled by this place, and as she took in the sight of the glorious heaven–like Presence that filled it, she marveled at the small pool of heaven's crystal sea, resident and flowing in the midst of this glorious place. She saw and felt in her physical body the colors of the rainbow floating in and out of the pool as it sparkled with a tranquil light emanating from within.

Breathtaking explosions of light lifted from it and seemed to take flight as though they were birthed from the power it possessed. And dancing in and out of it, tiny angelic beings enjoyed the atmospheric properties of the Presence, like young children enjoying the affection of their loving Father.

Wave after wave of brilliant splendor filled the old chapel and layered the atmosphere with heavenly substances. All at once, a tremendous wave of heightened glory reached out and struck Beloved, overwhelming her with its wonderment and she fell to her knees. Overpowered and undone by Him, her body lost its ability to stand.

As she fell to the floor, she saw circling all around the luminous pond the wonderfully alighted children. Not much older than the little boy who'd led her there, they seemed to be held captive. As if entranced, the children appeared as though they were a part of His effervescent glory. Yet, they seemed so familiar with the experience of His power, that, in seeing her need, they instantly leapt to help her.

Surrounding Beloved, the little ones were much stronger than they appeared and embraced her quickly to strengthen her. As her strength returned, they began pelting her with questions. "Who are you, lady?" they asked. "Are you the one the Father has sent to us? Are you the one we've been waiting for?" they bombarded her excitedly.

Altogether, there were a dozen children of varying ages, yet they seemed so much older than their years and had wisdom far greater than Beloved had detected in other much older seekers. Understandably so, for they had spent so much time in the presence of the Great Father they absorbed the Wisdom of the ages and, of course, had known she would be sent to them.

Beloved felt an inexpressible gratitude to the Father for having chosen to call her to this place. She knew instinctively these precious children were her assignment. In return, they would help *her* and the prophetic host in the impending battle to awaken His sleeping bride.

She felt in her spirit that He was, indeed, granting her such a tremendous honor as He appointed her to aid these truly *great saints*. How blessed and how delighted she was to be of help to them.

Overwhelmed by their vibrantly spirited hugs and kisses, she embraced them all as if she'd always known them, for she felt she always had.

"My dear, little friends," Beloved exclaimed, "the Father has great need of you. A fearsome battle is being fought now for possession of the earth. Your wisdom and your vivacious mercy is what He delights to gift to the prophetic host who need you desperately. And we do need you children, terribly. Will you come?"

She burst with pleasure to tell them of the Father's desire and without hesitation, the children agreed to go with her. A garden of big bright smiles stared back at her, expressing their great pleasure as they took on the spoken task the Father had designed for them. As a delightfully wise and intense feeling came over them, they seemed to grow in age even while she looked at them.

Beloved suddenly realized that having convinced them to accompany her, she did not know how she would convey them all to the quiet mountain. She had not yet given advanced thought to their next step.

Then it dawned on her: the Father's necessity would demand the help of the angelic. But as soon as she thought it, she'd seen that He'd already anticipated her need and saw to every detail without her realizing it. The cherished angelic who had been with the children and taken such blessed care of them thus far were overjoyed to transport them to the mountain's battle.

As if awaiting her need of them, the compliant angelic moved toward her to take up their needed positions. Beautifully, each angel wrapped themselves around a single child and lifted off into the chilled night's sky.

Beloved giggled with excitement as she realized what joy it was for the Father to use those whose hearts were bright with the young delight of faith. She understood then why the prophetic host had refused to receive her counsel.

Yes, the Father had a great work for her to undertake and she was overcome with joy by the task she had been given.

6

The Army of the Great

THE CHILDREN WERE absolutely thrilled as they rode with the angelic. They had never seen the world from flight's vantage point. As they flew, they reveled in the joy of everything they saw, for much of earth was brand new to them and some parts were still rather lovely.

Very few of the children had traveled far from the old school and they were filled with excitement. So much of the world was unfamiliar, and they were tickled over the changing scenery. Seeing it for the first time, they felt keenly the joy of their Father in His creation and believed quite rightly He'd created it just for them.

Beloved marveled at the easy rapport between the Elysian creatures who'd cared for them for so long in the old chapel and the children. Their relationship to all the elements of heaven's kingdom amazed her. Never one sided, she witnessed the genuine emotions the angelic felt for the children as well. They loved the children dearly and felt extremely close and beholden to them.

Naturally, they were overjoyed by the delight of the youngsters and wanted to prolong their time together for as long as they could. While they enjoyed touring mountain ranges, great rivers and the beautiful shores of the coastlines, they knew their flight would inevitably have to come to an end.

Although Beloved enjoyed the happy chatter of the young ones, she recalled the anxiousness of her friends. She did not trust that in their unfortunate impatience they would waste any time forming an army of their own. She felt uneasy about what she would find at the mountain when they arrived, so she pressed the group to hasten to their destination.

Reaching the base of the mountain, Beloved and

the children saw a large group of people gathered together in what appeared to them to be a celebration.

The angels deposited their cherished cargo near the expectant gathering. Tussling with each other, the children pushed against the crowd for a glimpse of what excited the multitude. All around them, they watched the crowd, trying to gain insight as to what they were waiting for.

Beloved could hardly keep up with them as they were overcome with excitement at seeing something new. Expecting to be a part of a terrible war, Beloved had led the children to believe they were dreadfully needed, which gave them all a feeling of importance and earnestness.

"What's to happen, Beloved?" Peter grabbed her hand urging her for an answer with his eyes.

Peter had become a special favorite of Beloved's and she desperately wished she could answer his troubled eyes with a brave response, but she herself did not know.

"I'm not at all sure," she answered with growing uneasiness.

Before either of them could ask further questions, a rustling sound reached them from a clearing in the forest near the base of the quiet mountain.

The crowd erupted as a gallant line of what appeared to be royalty burst through the forest. Their anticipated appearance heightened the excitement of the crowd, but it threw Beloved into emotional turmoil.

While her mind whirled with questions, the children beamed with unguarded excitement to see such a majestic display. Hanging on her arm, Peter looked at Beloved quite proudly, reassuring her he knew she understood what was taking place.

Along with the rest of the crowd, Beloved watched as a long line of soldiers dressed in mounted regalia cantered gallantly as if in a pre-war parade for a great battle. Arrayed royally in what seemed like medieval armor with gleaming silver helmets, heralding long, decorative feathers of great elegance, the army rode proudly on horseback above the cheering crowd.

The onlookers roared with excitement as they marveled at the impressive display of soldiers parading in front of them. Challenging the people to rise in faith at the sight of their power, they were cheered on by a very adoring crowd who had obviously placed all their trust in them. As the people reached almost a fever pitch in their excitement, Beloved felt they seemed to cheer them in relief of their willingness to battle for them so they would not have to fight themselves.

Watching in awe, Beloved felt the hope of the people rise with secured confidence as it filled the atmosphere. Their faith was obviously bolstered by the impressive brandishing of the tremendous army of the most powerful warriors in Christendom. Indeed, they strode with confidence and pride toward the impending battle with no doubts of their expected victory.

Bolstered by the praise of the people, they felt confident in themselves. They believed they had only to show up to the battle and they would naturally win. It was quite evident that the crowds of people felt the same. As the soldiers nodded toward the assemblages they passed, the gathering became even more enamored with the condescending greatness of the gallant warriors and roared with praise for them.

As they traveled past her, Beloved caught sight of the army they were to challenge. Off at a great distance, attempting to bar the entrance to the fields of grace, stood a foul, loathsome army. These contemptuous creatures were anxious to greet their challengers and, gleaming with repellant arrogance, were unimpressed by the grand regalia of their opponents.

Sneering and vomiting their venomous expletives in savory delight of their imminent fight and lining up with little to no fear of their adversaries, they were completely unaffected by the flamboyant parade in view.

Creatures hungry for destruction had only to wait for the army to come to them.

Most assuredly, bolstered by the applause of the people, the army gave a splendid display as they galloped boldly toward their impending victory. With the praise of the people filling their minds, they gave little thought to what they were approaching. The adoration of the people made them believe they were invincible.

Sitting tall and proud on their powerful steeds, the great warriors charged toward the demonic horde.

Very quickly, battle was underway.

Lunging and grunting, it soon became apparent how ill-equipped the warriors actually were. As the splendid soldiers were easily overwhelmed by the onslaught and each decidedly ripped from the saddles by the horde, they were caught horribly unaware.

Out-armed and out-manned, the army of the great was, in actuality, not nearly enough to take out the hordes of hell. Like bolstered lambs led to the slaughter, one important thing was blatantly wanting: humility. Its lacking was their horrible, unfortunate downfall, for the favor of God follows the *humble* and His favor carries His victory.

It was only a matter of minutes before the important army was overwhelmed and exhausted by the force of the dark army. Like vultures hungry for their prey, the army of the *great* was altogether too quickly consumed by their opponents.

Laying in heaps on the ground, their once beautiful armor was strewn all around them. Piles of silver mixed with fine weaponry were thrown off as worthless in scores covering the battlefield.

Crowds of astonished onlookers who had been captivated by the warriors stood stunned and frozen in demoralized amazement. Like lambs to the slaughter, the army of the *great* was led to believe they were great because they were the focus of so much adoration. The seekers had looked for their strength outside of themselves, in those they saw as "great" warriors instead of trusting in the power of the Father to be made manifest through *them.*

Shocked at their easy defeat, the crowd stood in disbelief. Rumblings of anger wafted through them. Unwilling to accept their failure, the crowd looked for someone to blame. Feeling let down, they questioned why they had lost, but one voice rose above the others.

"You have no one but yourselves to blame!" Beloved confronted them.

"You built these poor people up until they believed what you said about them. God didn't call them to fight this battle alone and you were not called to stand only on the sidelines and watch them win the victory for you. If you had fought with them by their side instead of idolizing them, they would not have fallen. You believed the lie that you were not powerful enough to fight in this battle, but this *was* your battle—yours and the Lord's. Humility is your shield and the Lord is your strength. Accept responsibility for your own actions, then receive the authority you lack," she reproved.

Unable to bear Beloved's chastisement, one man rose to counter her and spoke to the crowd. "Let's go and fight those devils now!" he screamed.

Attempting to raise again an atmosphere of presumptive victory, the man ran toward the now decimated battlefield and the crowd rose to follow him.

At a loss for what to do, they began to retrieve the armor of the fallen army in an attempt to arm themselves to fight the enemy. However, the misfitting armor left them frustrated and fearful as they didn't even know how to put it on. Untrained and ill-equipped, the throng was unrestrained and on the verge of furthering their disobedience.

Beloved was beside herself and in distress. Her heart cried to the Lord for His leading. Then she remembered her task, to find the children of His Presence. Would they have the answer?

It was the children who knew what to do. Their forthrightness disarmed the populace and they stepped back, away from the armor. Suddenly, for the first time, their attention was drawn to the children Beloved had brought with her.

One small boy of six stood up and hollered at the crowd, "No! No! This rubble is not for us! We've got *better armor!*"

Without discussing it first amongst themselves, the children hit the ground and began to pray. Assured that their example would be followed, they closed their eyes and focused their hearts toward the Father and the hushed crowd followed in utter amazement at the authority these small ones possessed.

Off in the distance, the once contemptuous horde felt a shutter run through their ranks. For the first time since the arrival of the army, they felt insecure in their stance against the host.

One vile demon was heard as he spit out violent threats at the existence of the children. Questioning his comrades, he wanted something to be done about them, but there was nothing that could be done to stop them. The children had come prepared to fight. Unlike Beloved's friends, they *had* sought the Lord before stepping into battle—they were prepared, and they were fearless.

Fear began to flood the horde as the children prayed. All the evil army could do was watch in fright as the skies above the children suddenly opened up to reveal the majestic, angelic creatures who had escorted them to their destination.

As if in response to the presence of the angelic, the children were filled with immediate understanding as they watched the descending angelic approach the needy crowd carrying robes of pure white liquid glory.

Dressing the assemblage, they armed them with the power of heaven's authority and instantly felt empowered and filled with understanding as well.

One by one, the people were arrayed in simple robes of glory. They paid little attention to the look or power of their robes. No one compared themselves to others, for the glory had captivated their souls and they moved together in one spirit, with one goal. Instantly, their presumption was subdued. Their focus was fixed on the chore at hand as the Spirit of the Lord turned their attention once again toward the demonic horde.

With the vast army turning toward them in ardent earnestness, the demonic horde was suddenly consumed by a desperate, unearthly, supernatural fear.

From just a plain, simple army of men, women and children dressed in glory, these terrible creatures turned and ran in all directions. And as they ran, the people chased them for a time, but then eventually stopped to watch them run.

One little girl ran after them and screamed, "And don't you come back, ya hear?!"

Forming a crowd around the children, the grateful throng embraced one another in celebration of the victory, which clearly only God had given them. Open access to the fields of grace was theirs once more.

Beloved nearly burst with pride over how well *her* children had led during the battle. She was overjoyed at the Lord's gift to her of this powerful army of children. She felt triumphant hope rise in her heart as she was guided by Holy Spirit, her friend and constant Companion.

However, feeling the urging of the Great One, the angelic who'd guided the children pressed them to rush to the mountain of the Lord.

"There's no time to be wasted," they urged. "The armies of heaven are preparing to enter the spirit-realm of earth. You must find shelter in the presence of the Most High."

After boldly fighting and gaining their first real victory, Beloved and the children left the battle scene and scampered to ascend the mountain of the Lord. Together, with the crowd of seekers, they were weary from their experience on the battlefield and the climb was taking a toll on them. Eventually, they neared the rim of the flattop mountain, but felt exhausted and hindered by their rushed climb to safety.

Beloved knew she must allow the children to rest a bit and settled herself in a safe spot to watch over them. Standing near them, she turned in expectation toward the battlefield they'd left.

"Nothing yet," she thought. *"We still have*

time... "she reassured herself.

Then, turning back to the children, something caught her attention.

A single white feather floated down and lay at her feet. Reaching to pick it up, she marveled at its simple beauty. Stunned by its perfection, she examined every barb while it glistened as if it radiated the power of the sun from within its rachis.

Wondering where it had come from, she looked up. Above her, to her amazement, the skies were teeming with the angelic.

Monopolizing the sky overhead, each heavenly creature was different and yet fitted together perfectly with the other, enhancing their stately magnificence. Gentle, yet intensely warlike, they manifested their Father's protective care for the host and the children of His Presence.

"Truly," Beloved thought, *"the Father has kept His heavens right with us all the time. He's never left us alone... We've never been alone..."*

7

Wave of Salt

EMBOLDENED BY THE SIGHT of the angel-filled sky, they shouted out for His will to become manifest on earth. Over and over they called to the Father, "On earth as it is in heaven!" as if by their words they were giving birth to the declarations of their Savior!

As their cry rose, they were prodigiously joined by the armies of heaven in their joyful declaration. "Yes, God!" they shouted together, "On earth as it is in heaven!"

Again and again, heaven and earth joined in

unison resounding in a truly joyous decree until, at last, their Father, bursting with joyful pride, answered their cry with a cry of His own.

His voice, the voice of a thousand thunders, cracked and roared throughout the sky above the quiet mountain and encircled it with the powerful fiery breath of His voice... like the voice of the ocean crashing against a thousand seashores.

"RELEASE!" the Father roared into the atmosphere encircling the earth.

Penetrating the light of the photosphere, His words created a corona hole sending His breath upon the earth like an echo pounding into its depths and shaking its foundations.

From the safety of the mountaintop, the warriors stood watching in breathless expectancy as they viewed the horizons far off in the distance.

From every corner of the universe, His roar was heard, permeating the oceans of earth and shattering the stillness of the mountain, causing it to shudder with its force.

The oceans shook and trembled, waters roared and foamed and from the mouth of the ocean rose an army of pure white horses numbering in the millions. As if created from the foam of the water, united by His presence, the horses fought the grip of the waters to reach the shores of earth, bursting forth with great force as they reached land.

Seeming to leap onto the surface of the planet, they were resolute in their assigned task: to prepare this world for what it was about to receive from God.

This mighty herd pelted the earth with their hooves, resounding like the beat of a thousand drums all playing in unison like a cannonade of drumfire.

Fear gripped the inhabitants of earth's realm as, again and again, the horses covered every inch of it. Nothing was left untouched by this great army. Over and over, they drove their hooves into the earth, each time causing great tremors throughout.

Beloved watched as the horses pounded the ground, and felt fear for earth's inhabitants. *"For, surely,"* she thought, *"nothing could survive this mighty assault."*

Just then, a great shout of joy was heard throughout the universe as the warriors in both realms saw the goodness of their Father displayed for all the world to see.

A revolution was beginning...

All eyes seemed to turn in unison to the waters of the ocean. Infused with the power from the Father's own throne and filled with salt and light, a giant wave rose high in the sky, formed from the waters of the oceans. Higher and higher it rose, as the warriors rejoiced, until finally the wave seemed to come alive with the same joy that filled the well-loved saints.

As the height of the wave reached the circumference of the earth, it began to fall, slowly at first and then with a mighty crash, penetrating every region of the earth's surface. Overwhelming it with the salt and light it possessed, it broke down upon the darkness all over the world. For a moment, the inhabitants of the earth were stunned and could do nothing in response to the wave's power.

All the earth experienced the salt and light of heaven—every soul felt the reality of heaven fall upon them.

Beloved knew the sleeping bride, the lost and everyone on earth would feel this moment—the Father's moment. No matter how they chose to live in the future, they could not deny they had experienced this moment. Truly, this was the point in time they felt His truth, as they were indeed captivated by the power of it.

After all they had been told, they would experience truth—the truth that God *is real.* They would have to deal with the sudden and powerful reality they'd tried to suppress.

Every soul would have to choose. Would they receive Him and humble themselves, or revile Him and revolt?

Pulsating through mountains, valleys and terrain, the wave filled the earth with its compounds. Pounding like the beating of a heart, the salt and light were alive with heaven's glorious joy. Falling on man and beast, it broke over them as though it were breaking chains of captivity and releasing its breathtaking reign of light.

Pulsing, breathing and giving life as it cascaded through the earth on a quest to release the Father's great joy, His mysterious plan culminated into a spectacular display of His power. He was, indeed, *real*.

His warriors knew their lives would never be the same and the earth would be ignited by the fire of His truth until all the kingdoms of this world bowed to Him.

The roots of unbelief were targeted first by the wave of His salt, purifying the strains of disparaging lies about God's home, His people, Himself and His power. Although some may choose in the end not to serve Him or love Him, they may not receive Him, but there would be no doubt that they would know of His existence.

Beloved and the host knew there would be only a short time to work and they must act now to use the Father's gift. Each knew his place and ran to release the callings they possessed. Though they would be apart in the natural, they were as one in the Spirit.

They felt a clearness in their thinking they'd never felt before and their love and appreciation for one another increased with it. Any fear or envy was quickly washed away. In its place, they felt increased passion to have His will on the earth as it is experienced in heaven.

This was their moment; the Father had given it to them.

The washing of the wave would strengthen their boldness and their faith, purifying them all from the residue of unbelief as they rushed to take their places in the display of His glory on the earth. Many who were feeling His Presence for the first time were afraid of what they were feeling and would need the peace of His understanding.

And so Beloved rose up and addressed the crowds of the awakened. "We are now entering a time of unprecedented supernatural war in the heavenlies between the kingdom of Light and the kingdom of darkness. It is the kingdom of our Father warring against the dark kingdoms on this earth—pulling down strongholds that have plagued this world for centuries.

"Our enemy has attempted to rule over us in an effort to thwart the worship of God's creation and suck the life from His children. But he has failed! And now, the King of heaven will enter the realms of earth and begin a major spiritual war to buckle the gates of the enemy's defenses and establish the government of His kingdom on earth in us.

"God's supernatural war is heightening and the Lord is calling for His watchmen to ask the Father to establish His government in themselves. As He is glorified in them, the Light of His kingdom will dawn on the earth and be established in it as it is in heaven.

"As His bride, we will literally be transformed! Through His liquid glory, He will transform us into the most breathtaking, captivating bride ever imagined. This glorious, beautiful church will rise and rule in His power and the world will be amazed.

"Our inheritance is waiting..."

As she was speaking, a shadow fell over the earth, the shadow of another mighty wave. It rose like a great storm cloud, growing darker and darker until, at last, it too crashed over the earth. The crowd watched in earnest as the wave curled upward, finally turning into a massive arm and looking just like an arm as it is flexed. This was the Arm of the Lord.

As His massive arm struck the earth, the ground trembled under the weight of it. Beloved watched as everywhere it touched down a powerful mountain arose. The mountains grew and grew until they were higher than any of earth's mountains, making them seem like small hills in comparison. Fearing first the shadow the wave brought, Beloved expected something ominous and fearful, yet she felt the Lord speak to her, "Every storm cloud seems dark and fearful, but the wise will learn to anticipate the rain."

He continued, "My wave, My shadow and My arm bring My fear. I am reestablishing My fear upon the earth. A holy awe—the fear of the Lord. I will reveal My power to My enemies.

"It is true, fear of My judgment is the beginning of all other wisdom. They must first know I exist, that I am God and that I rule or they will be lost; fearing Me as God gives them a compass to navigate through this war. If they know I exist, they will be forced to choose Me or deny Me. They will, indeed, see ME and then they must choose."

Beloved turned to the miraculous mountain the Father created and saw that He had named it. He called it, "UNDENIABLE."

"If they turn away from Me at this point, there can be no escape from the coming judgment, for I have made Myself known to them; they have seen Me and cannot deny that I exist—I AM REAL."

"I have come in answer to the prayers and hunger of My people. For the faithful, I am Faithful. But to the devious, I will manifest as Shrewd.

"The oppressors of My people, the thieves that have robbed them, are symptoms of the lack of fear My people have for Me—even My church. The symptoms of abortion, greed, perversion and idolatry have grown in this world because My people have perceived evil to be good. They've lost their compass, which is their fear of Me. As they perceive My power, they will again stand in great AWE of Me.

"Just like Israel learned to be ashamed of their behavior, so, too, will this world suddenly see and bear the shame of their previous behavior. This disgrace will either bring them near Me, seeking forgiveness or they will harden their hearts and try to run from Me.

"There will be a genuine outcry for purity and holiness among My people. Even the harvesters of the enemy's lies will suddenly be captivated by My power. And they, too, will feel the shame of their past betrayal and will seek out My true followers for deliverance.

"Those in My church who only pretend to know Me will experience gut-wrenching repentance. Those who've used My church as a weapon or a tool to build for themselves and My enemy will be stunned by the sudden reality of the light of My presence.

"My captives will be released and My servants will come to know themselves as I know them and nothing will again stop them."

Suddenly, Beloved remembered the Lord had said in Isaiah 10:24-27, "O my people in Zion, do not be afraid of the Assyrians when they oppress you with rod and club as the Egyptians did long ago. In a little while My anger against you will end, and then My anger will rise up to destroy them.

The Lord of Heaven's armies will lash them with His whip, as He did when Gideon triumphed over the Midianites at the rock of Oreb, or when the Lord's staff was raised to drown the Egyptian army in the sea. In that day, the Lord will end the bondage of His people. *He will break the yoke of slavery and lift it from their shoulders.*"

With sudden understanding, Beloved and the people were truly beginning to realize the fear of the

Lord was a great treasure, without which there is no guide to life.

Amongst themselves, they discussed His revelations, and the impact was felt deeply. Truly they discovered He was a loving Father and as such seeks to guide them. Yearning to please their well-beloved Father, they were guided by His wisdom. Embracing His truth with true awe of the coming day of judgment, they understood, *it is those who've embraced His fear who will have nothing to fear.* He will be their Triumph and Deliverer.

And those who have been held captive by the bondage of the world will have the opportunity to accept His freedom—releasing the return of His prodigals to the care of His bride.

As the host rested in His words, they realized their treasure would be the fear of the Lord, for they would fear *nothing but Him.* As He spoke, a verse of scripture sprang into Beloved's heart and she remembered, *"The fear of the Lord will be your **treasure**"* *Isaiah 33:6.*

His Spirit speaking to hers, Beloved realized it was the awe of God which births humility, and humility brings forth miracles.

She was then taken up by the Spirit into another

realm...

8

His Deliverance

TAKEN OUT OF the physical realm of earth, Beloved was in a place she'd never seen before. She stood alone on what seemed to her a vast sea of scorched, desolate ground. It was resolutely the most barren place she'd ever been. The sky above was filled with a dusty orange haze, permeating the hopeless atmosphere that filled the desperate place. She was sure nothing ever could nor ever had grown in such a spiritless land.

Unsure of why she was there, she knew this realm was the *spirit-realm hovering over the earth* and she guardedly observed her surroundings with the effort of a vigilant surveyor. Reassuring herself that the Father would never permit any harm to come to her, she tried in vain to let her instinctive guard down.

She saw movement on the horizon. Something very small and dark seemed to be crawling toward her on the ground.

Relieved, Beloved heaved a panic-eased sigh of relief. "It's only a spider..." she whispered to herself. "A little larger than usual, but only a spider."

Still, her spirit continued to deduce a keen sense of alertness in the surroundings, but she was trying to convince herself there was no need to be alarmed.

Yet as she watched the horizon, a few more eight-legged creatures followed the path of the one preceding them. Curious, but not alarmed, Beloved noticed farther out on the parched dry field even more spiders.

Her hard-won peace was very soon bruised by the rising realization that it wasn't just a few large spiders, but was quickly becoming a horde... all headed toward her.

Rapidly, the scene before her changed to one that equaled the alarm in her spirit. She was suddenly being overrun by black, wiry, tittering spiders.

Beloved did not know what to make of what

was happening and was unsure if she was truly in danger. Suddenly, she realized it was, in fact, *millions* of spiders running, racing toward her, all around. Soon, she could see nothing now but arachnidian, and they were almost on top of her. Quite shocked, she quickly turned in an attempt to run away, but soon realized she was running *with* them, not away.

As she second-guessed her impulse to run, she turned back in time to catch a glimpse of something that took her breath away.

Shocked, Beloved froze for a moment, trying to see more clearly what she hoped she did not see. She stopped and gazed into the distance from where they appeared to have come from.

Beloved gasped.

She now realized the spiders were not running *at her,* but were running *from* something. They were running at a terrified speed from an enormous, rolling cloud of thick heavy dust and smoke that was fast approaching!

Beloved watched in terror as she felt physically frozen, unable to move. She was stunned by what appeared to her as a massive, rushing dust cloud, preparing to engulf her.

White smoke exploded repeatedly from the cloud as if it were alive. Rolling powerfully toward her, she instinctively felt the fury of the inferno it possessed as explosions of energy within shifted its force like a steering wheel, steadying its path.

As fear increased amongst the spiders all around her, Beloved's weak hold on peace was dissipating. She was now overcome by dread, fearing for her life.

Just as she had braced herself for the inevitable end, she saw a vague glimmer of something emerging from the depth of the cloud.

Beloved fixed her eyes straight into it.

Trying to convince herself she did, indeed, see what she had thought she'd seen, the emergent revealed itself again.

Yes. She was sure now. She had truly seen a human form rising from the center of the billowing mass. Leaping and bounding in the raging inferno of monumental dust and energy was the figure of a man.

The closer the cloud drew, the more clearly she saw the image of a man riding on a powerful, massive horse, bounding toward her with such force it shook the ground as it landed. Over and over, like the power in a great engine, the horse and rider closed in on the dreadful spiders. Again and again, they gained ground and Beloved realized they, with all their might, would soon be upon her as well.

In her mesmerized state, she'd not taken the time to answer the questions of her own heart, but instinctively started to run away as earnestly and desperately as the hopelessly tormented creatures had.

Running breathlessly for her life, Beloved did not know how long she had run before the creeping realization passed over her that it was utterly fruitless and she began to slow. Her curiosity grew beyond what she could hold back. She decided she must know.

Who was riding the massive beast?

Suddenly, as she tested her thoughts, a refuge seemed to appear out of nowhere and Beloved climbed atop a great rock seemingly provided for her safety. Bounding to the top of the rock, she leapt with intensity and, catching her breath, turned impatiently to watch the massive cloud with horse and Rider approach.

From this vantage point, she no longer considered fear. Her entire being was filling now with the wonder of the reality pouring out before her.

Truly, it was *He.* She knew His form and ruddy-brown hair. And given away by His steady resolve, she well recognized Him and was instantly filled with relieved anticipation.

Joy consumed her entire being. She was overcome with rapture, for riding on a massive white horse came a king...*her King!* Wearing a thick gold crown, His hair blew about from His erratic charge, creating the thick cloud as He rode.

She stared intensely. "His eyes, I must see His eyes!"

Suddenly, Beloved saw His face, reddish-brown, peering from beneath the fog of smoke and dust, and in an instant her heart jumped in her chest.

His *eyes...*

Piercing her like lightning striking a lifeless soul, it was then she realized how much death had penetrated her life on earth. His eyes possessed the treasure of heaven, the glory of the domains of His Father. Ferocious, fiery eyes, He was the terror of hell—the unstoppable Fearsome of heaven's realm. And HE had come to earth...

She had seen Him before, yes, but not here. She'd not seen the Fire of Heaven in this desolate, dark spirit-realm and He took her breath away. All her fears vanished, replaced by the intensity of every dream she'd ever dreamt coming to a sudden and powerful reality before her.

"My Lord!" she felt herself scream with all her

might into the tornado of dust approaching her.

Turning to her in response, she saw hundreds of watchers surrounding the Lord, appearing to her like glimmers of light reflecting a celestial glow. Now she could see again the angelic filling the sky all around Him.

His ride continued violently, dust exploding, while flashes of fire followed all around as He rode. Like a violent storm, He made His advance toward the parched, dry fields of the earth.

Charging to meet His accusers, and those of His well-loved bride, the Rider approached.

Generating a massive storm as He entered earth's atmosphere, sundering the strongholds tightly held by the enemy for generations, He broke through their intensely strong grip as though it were nothing. Devastating the earth's surface with the great noise of its massive hooves, the white horse and Rider thundered through the dry, dense earth.

Followed by the horse's forceful gallop, Beloved saw words emerging from its hooves each time they landed. Like swords penetrating the hard earth, powerful words crashed through the ground like lightning. Beloved knew she must focus on the words.

Again and again, like the barrage from a great

army, the words cut through the earth's crust, penetrating through it to its core. It was His Word!

They were King David's words. She recognized them from the Psalms.

Over and over, they pounded through the earth. Unshakable in their retribution, they tore into the depths of the dust: *"But the wicked will die. The Lord's enemies are like flowers in a field – they will disappear like smoke." (Psalm 37:20)*

"The wicked draw their swords and string their bows to kill the poor and the oppressed, to slaughter those who do right." (v. 14)

On and on the words struck the earth like the fist of God, *"But their swords will stab their own hearts, and their bows will be broken." (v. 15)*

Reaching out like tentacles underground, the light-filled words penetrated the earth with the truth of the inescapable retribution of the Lord of heaven's armies. *"The strength of the wicked will be shattered..." (v. 17)* Beloved felt faint from the intensity of their power.

Collapsing onto the rock where she had been standing, she held herself in check. *"Don't,"* Beloved coached herself. *"You're not going to fail Him now! He needs you!"*

On and on He rode over the earth, generating

87

strong earth-shattering quakes throughout the earth. Beloved was girded in strength by the unseen force of her Holy Guide. As she steadied herself, she wanted to imprint the image on her mind.

All around her, she felt the demonic forces of evil scamper in terror as He rode. It was *their* terror she'd felt. They had expected this all along and yet, they had grown lethargic in their watch of Him.

Filled with the dread of doom, they could only flee in terror as they were shaken by His sudden approach. Flooded with panic, the scourge of spiders felt the force of His Words pounding into the earth.

Riding over the surface of the supernatural field, Beloved watched as He was joined by many others. Those who'd been martyred for His sake rode with Him as He drove His massive army over the surface of the earth.

He rode ceaselessly until, at last, He felt He'd covered the vast territory and came to an awe-inspiring halt.

Surrounded by a glory cloud, the White Horse Rider appeared as though riding in a celestial nebulous glow, with fiery clouds and swirling mists of purple, red, blue and bright fuchsia rolling continuously in and around Him. Endlessly, the sounds of crashing water flooded the sky. He seemed to break through the barrier of the earth's realm as easily as stepping through a door.

As lightning struck out from Him, the sky continued to break with cracks of thunder. The nebulae swirled around Him like a imposing group of creatures breathing in and out. Fire-like stars burst in and through Him as He stood radiantly regal in the midst of the natural realm's sky.

Robed like a bear, with the mane of a lion draped around His shoulders and chest, His garment trailed behind him, blanketing the great, white, warrior-horse He rode. Flowing like fiery blood into the nebulous surrounding him, the Rider steadied His steed as the great horse grew fiercely impatient after its charge.

Intensely anxious to accomplish his task, the extraordinary beast beat his hooves upon the ground again and again, releasing even more powerful earthquakes into the earth. As clouds of fire burst from his nostrils as he heaved, he bared his teeth like an animal ready to strike.

Atop the head of the White Horse Rider was a tremendous gleaming crown mounted like a sky scraper of golden towers and His eyes were flames of white fire.

When He looked at her, Beloved felt

overwhelmed by the power of His unspeakable *love.*

9

THE WHITE
HORSE RIDER

STANDING FIRM OVER the firmament of the
earth, the great King held His place as He
transformed the skies around Him. Revealing itself
from the center of the cloud was the formation of an
army of white warriors. Riding with Him, all around
Him, His army emerged as a great mountain. As if
stepping out of the heavenlies into earth's realm, it
seemed to frame Him like the landscape from an
awe-inspiring portrait.

He held His place in steady resolve as the vast wave of riding warriors swirled around Him, riding on the fiery nebula generated by the glory of their King. Altogether, His army watched, intently waiting for even a hint of direction from the Rider in anticipation of their impending attack.

Beloved timidly observed the White Horse Rider as He gauged the scene. He'd seen the kingdoms of the dark realm standing proudly in defiance against His majesty. And yet, now as Beloved watched, she saw a fiery bolt of concentrated anger fill His chest.

Building in intensity until it burst forth out of His mouth like the roar of a thousand lions, this roar-like fire produced a sharp penetrating sound. This utterance brought forth a sword from His mouth that would invade even the most remote and imbedded strongholds of the kingdoms of darkness. Seeming to explode with the force of His rage, the powerful, glistening sword erupted from His throat.

As it charged toward His enemies, the great sword split itself into thousands of smaller swords flying in every direction all around Him. Panicked with no escape, the enemy's terror did not last long. Utterly disintegrating their long-held enchantments, His swords reached them. Enveloped with a power much greater than that of even a nuclear blast, the swords filled the air with dread.

As fear grew in the troll-like, impish creatures guarding the kingdoms of the dark realm, there was no time for them to brace themselves or understand what was happening. As an intense terror filled them entirely, they and the mighty, dark towers of their realm vanished, literally incinerated in a brief moment.

All over the field of battle, this scene was repeated by the multiplied tens of thousands. As each sword flew, watchers went with it. Like a streak of fire in the sky, they guided each sword toward its destination, for they were jubilant with desire to take part in the joy of victory. Making sure it reached its mark, they wanted to record the destruction of their enemies.

Beloved had known for some time this engagement would take place. It was the Lord's battle to awaken His bride.

Truly, He had come to destroy the realms of darkness holding the bride in the grip of the deep sleep.

Suddenly, this unearthly, holy army came to a standstill. In its entirety, they turned their attention to Beloved. Trying to hide in the shadows cast from the light of the fiery cloud, she realized she was now wearing a white chiffon gown that shown bright with His reflected glory like a diamond reflects the light. Time seemed to come to a halt all around her while this powerful army stood in expectancy as the Rider's glory-cloud rolled into itself like a mighty wave in a storm. Holding the army in its grasp, the celestial nimbus rolled in all directions inside of itself and trailed out around them at a great distance as they traveled.

Every wave of the cloud seemed to have a life of its own, yet rolled violently throughout each other to generate a boundless yet fierce nimbus glow. Visible crowns of light-filled fog reflected off human faces, which seemed to flow in and out of the cloud, only occasionally visible to her.

Escorted by the fires of another realm, she again caught sight of her King. She was instantly captivated by His powerful gaze, but felt overwhelmed in the grasp of its intensity.

Understandingly, His intensity gave way to an easier expression until, at last, He smiled at her.

Catching her breath, she smiled back.

"Beloved," He spoke to her. His voice still reverberated through the atmosphere like the storm clouds that roared around Him, overpowering her natural senses as He spoke. "It is time now."

She answered Him timidly, "Time, Lord?"

Smiling at her again, now with even greater joy, He seemed to speak to her as though He were a thousand voices and yet, only one. "Beloved, this is what you asked me for."

She suddenly realized what He was offering her and almost replied back before He finished, "It is time for you to ride with me, Beloved..."

She instantly understood as she recalled a memory from a dream and she began to tremble. Gathering herself together to stand before Him, she saw Him reach out His hand to collect her in His arms.

The great horse steadied itself to receive its precious passenger as she was gently nestled in front of her Lord. The cloud, too, seemed to anticipate and receive her into itself, as a swift current of energy rolled through it. This was truly the great joy of our Lord, to receive His Beloved unto Himself.

The fire cloud seemed to react to the Lord's joy as she leaned back on His chest. She gained an easy repose as her gown blew out all around her as they rode. Her lengthy sleeves trailed down the sides of the great beast, entwining with the horses white mane, glowing as the light-filled power of the beast wafted through them.

She never wanted the moment to end, yet she knew this was only the beginning for her. What she'd been waiting for and praying for was in the near future. For her, and for the Lord's seekers, things were about to change.

Filled with the thoughts that seemed to pervade the cloud, Beloved's mind was occupied with the memory of the armies preparing for heaven's war. The Holy Spirit's wisdom invaded Beloved's mind. While she rested in Her Lord's arms, the King shared the secrets of the *future battle for His bride's heart.*

As she rode with Him, He invaded her thoughts with powerful impressions of tenderness as she relaxed into His chest.

IO

GOD'S ROBE

TRANSFORMING THE SKYLINE, the Father entered the atmosphere and filled the earth with Himself. Warm and inviting, He watched and waited for His children to come to Him. He wore a long and glorious light-filled robe, rays of light emanating from it as it bathed the landscape with His glory.

Captivated by the Father's robe, Beloved discovered this was no ordinary garment—it was adorned and embellished with nothing less than human souls. Seemingly embroidered and woven into the fabric of the Father's glorious robe, He'd chosen to grace Himself in a raiment of the people He loved.

Like any good father would, He loved to show off His *robe of treasure,* as He called it. As He did, the Father slowly twirled around to reveal all the many people and ministries in it that reached all over the world declaring and sharing the glory of His kingdom.

Beloved loved watching as He danced to reveal the splendor of His prized garment. As the seekers worshiped and rejoiced in Him, His robe was made brighter even more so than before. As those He loved delighted in Him, the train of His glory lengthened and fell well below His feet.

He chose to dress Himself in people, all people, from all nations—those who were found by Him and chose to live in Him. Radiantly, they beamed with His power flowing through them. They were, indeed, overjoyed to be a part of His precious garment.

Proud to reveal the people He loved and their breathtaking splendor, He beamed with joy and pride as He turned around and around, slow at first and then a bit faster. As He twirled, His robe of people swirled out from around Him and it increased and grew until it reached all over the globe.

His eternal-robe knocked down mountains and kingdoms of the earth, leveling any that had been made by man's design, which were raised to draw others to the temporal beauty of creation. It obliterated the idols of man, which He especially hated because they distracted the people from Him and kept them from receiving His love.

Around and around He turned, until the glory from His robe covered the earth and the earth glowed with His resplendence.

He stopped and turned His back toward Beloved and she watched as He manifested His robe like a mighty mountain. He wanted her to see the countless people trying in vain to climb the back of His robe to get to the top of the mountain, not realizing *He was the mountain.*

The soul-lined robe was simply unrecognizable to those whose only thoughts were manipulated by ambitions of self-grandeur. As they tried to climb the mountain of God's robe, they did not even see that the gems they were climbing on were actually human souls—their brothers and sisters in Christ.

Using the precious people within His robe to anchor and steady themselves for the climb, they pulled and stepped on them as though they were only rock. Climbing sometimes for years, these ambitious brothers and sisters used the humble, yet beautiful gem-souls as though they had no other value except for their usefulness to the climbers.

Of course, those ascending caused those they stepped on great pain, but, mysteriously, the Lord allowed it to happen. Pushing and clambering, the ambitious revealed their hearts to the Lord and as they did, He could see they were not yet ready to become a part of Him. He watched the climbers patiently as they damaged His beautiful robe, but He never lost heart. He waited patiently for them to become more desperate for Him.

However, focused only on the climb, living on Him, but not *in Him,* the ambitious often fell, especially when the Father gave a little shudder of His back, shaking many climbers loose. It was His mercy toward them as they tumbled back down to the bottom of His mountainous robe. It pleased Him to do it, because their focus was not what it should be—they were missing the joy He was offering them. And what a fall some of them had, for He was, indeed, a tall mountain.

Only those souls who were embedded *into* His robe could withstand the movement of it. They were held secure, woven into the very fibers of His raiment. They seemed to even glisten with His joy as

He shuffled His back to show Beloved that no one who climbs can stay, only those who choose to be a part of Him will endure.

Shining more brightly, those who dwelt in His robe radiated even brighter during these moments, and as they did, even those who'd fallen off while trying to climb watched them in wonder. For some of the climbers, it was the first time they'd considered the value of the gem-souls and it brought them much needed revelation of the Father's love.

Passing by all the vast wealth of treasure in His robe, the ambitious didn't see the value in souls and used them instead of cherishing them. Thoughtlessly climbing, they knew they were called, but didn't yet understand what true greatness was.

Beloved realized the Father didn't mind that they would climb on Him; He seemed to expect it. And when one climber would suddenly open His eyes and awaken to the reality of the robe-mountain, the entire robe would erupt with great joy. Radiating the light of their value, the gem-souls came alive when even just one climber saw their true worth.

Such wealth lay in store for those who discovered the Father's treasured gems. Earlier, as they had been busy climbing, they had seen these individual souls as valueless, foolish people who did not matter. The climbers saw them as less, because they were not as ambitious as they were and considered them lazy and undeserving because they lacked the ambition to climb.

However, after a fall, many began to see them differently. Beginning to understand, they saw the gems as *true* followers, because they did not use God to get higher, but chose to live in Him and to become a part of Him.

With newly contrite hearts, they could suddenly see the gem-souls as if they had just revealed themselves from all areas over His robe. However, it was the Father who revealed them to the previously ambitious climbers. Truly, although the gem-souls had been there all along, they were not visible to those climbing until the climbers were humiliated by their own fall.

Some, however, refused to acknowledge the gem-souls, choosing instead to harden their hearts, missing entirely the great treasure of the Father. The treasures of humility and meekness were disregarded by the vain, self-centered travelers, who even saw the gem-souls as lesser Christians.

Beloved watched as the climbers mocked them, seeing them as lazy, small and insecure. In shock, Beloved watched as the rebellious, finally seeing the gem-souls, dishonored them instead of seeing the value the Father put on them. Some even saw them as anti-Christians who got in God's way; they felt that in kicking the gem-souls, they were serving God.

Beloved tried to make them hear her as she held tightly to the Lord for strength. "Can't you see? You are kicking God! He is the Robe! He is the Mountain! The gem-souls are HIM!" she cried out.

Turning to the Rider, she buried her face in Him! Moved by her tender heart, He explained, *"This is the Father's choice; it's the ramifications of His merciful heart. He chooses to give them time to see. This period of mercy in the lives of the selfish is especially important to Him, for many have turned to Him even after years of blindness."*

Returning her attention to the Father's robe, Beloved began to understand the process mercy takes in a human soul, and understood that *mercy never gives up*.

For those climbers who were able to see them, the gem-souls, in turn, threw down ropes for the climbers to use. However the ropes did not lead *up*, but *into* the robe of God. In their humbled condition, the climbers were grateful to receive the help and did as they were told.

Grasping tightly to the mercy ropes, they held on as they were pulled in and out of the fibers of the robe. Although this was a long and tedious process, sometimes requiring years of patience for them, they were overjoyed to encounter the realms of the Father they had previously doubted existed.

Continually asked to submit to Father's leadership regardless of the cost, they chose to lay down what they'd previously deemed priceless. What they felt they could not live without had now become *nothing* in comparison to *living in Him*.

The Father's great mystery began to take shape as the climbers were woven in and out, shoved through the fibers of God's robe. Each time they endured His handiwork, they were cleansed ever so much more by the fibers of His glory-robe. Without realizing it, the fibers of His robe were cleansing the dross from their souls, over and over again. Each time they experienced the immense and wondrous cleansing of their souls, they became more *like Him*.

Sometimes, when they thought they had finally settled into place, they were suddenly moved again. Often in their journey, as they were tempted to give up, the fibers of His garment seemed to change and become much softer, more pliable and comfortable than before.

Lower and then higher, in and out, they were moved until, at last, they were fastened securely in Him. It was then they realized they too were one of the Father's treasured gem-souls, shiny and bright, glistening in the light of their Father's glory.

Contrite, cleansed and polished, they were securely fitted and nestled in the position the Father created for each of them, as though it had been made with them in mind. They were truly needed and were celebrated by the family of God's garment! They finally felt the belonging their soul yearned for.

As the Lord revealed the mystery of the Father to her, Beloved finally understood the secret of His woven masterpiece—the glorious mountainous robe He'd designed Himself—and she didn't want the moment to end. All the challenges she faced in her life, the times she'd felt abandoned by Him, suddenly made sense and she reveled in the joy of her Father's great love.

She was discovering the mysterious plan of our Father—to create a family from His fallen creation—was even more of a miracle of mercy than creation itself. Redeeming a fallen world is an even greater example of who the Father is than discarding them and starting afresh. Beloved realized that endeavoring to understand the Father is to comprehend the greatest mystery the world has ever known.

Still resting in her Lord's arms, she felt the Rider breathe the secrets of her destiny into her spirit. More than ever before, she was excited and thrilled, for her future would, indeed, hold the answers to her heart's greatest joy. Her heart desperately longed to fight for those who were in most need of her help, and now she knew what she would do next.

She would return to the *river of shame!*

In Closing

THE FATHER IS anxiously awaiting the Revolution of those He calls His Beloved, redeeming this world and those He loves from His enemy is our Father's greatest dream. He is exceedingly eager for the world He loves so much to know what He is really like, to know Him as He is. Like us, He too yearns to be understood and for love of Him, that is our task.

It is my expressed desire that *Revolution: The White Horse Rider* has brought you greater revelation of your heavenly Father. Like the parables of Jesus, this vision seeks to reveal His heart to the world so we might share Him as He truly is to a world which desperately needs Him.

Our great joy is also our commission from the Lord. We must do all we can in these last hours to know Him rightly and to, indeed, make Him know.

His mercy triumphs!

Have You Read...

The first installment of The Deep Sleep Trilogy: With the fate of the world in the balance, Beloved must rise above the deceptive snares of her adversaries to fulfill her calling: to pursue the prophetic host and liberate the slumbering army of the Lord. Destined to wage war against the darkness, the army must be awakened to destroy the enemy's grasp on the world.

OTHER BOOKS BY VICTORIA BOYSON:

The Birth of Your Destiny: Just like a baby hidden in the womb, so are the promises God has given to us. He speaks to us of our future as if to conceive within us His will and purpose for our lives. Experience an impartation of God's grace and faith to fulfill all that God has for you through this powerful and insightful book.

His Passionate Pursuit: Victoria challenges you to embrace the captivating revelations of His passion for you—His beloved bride. It is an invitation to an awakening encounter with God. His Passionate Pursuit is a portal to heaven, unleashing God's presence into your life, empowering you with an impartation from His heart.

God's Magnum Opus: The Value of a Woman: God loved Adam so much, He created the greatest, most inspiring work of art He could for him—Eve! She was the expression of the Father's love. A priceless treasure, indeed! In woman, the Father created His Magnum Opus, His work of art—the grand finale of His creation masterpiece. In the Father's grand design for humanity, *you* are His magnum opus!

To contact the author or to order more copies of REVOUTION: THE WHITE HORSE RIDER, please visit Victoria's website at www.VictoriaBoyson.com.

REVOUTION: THE WHITE HORSE RIDER is also available through Amazon.com, Christian bookstores and other online bookstores. It is also available as an eBook, purchasable through Amazon.com.

You can follow Victoria Boyson on Facebook, Twitter and Goodreads.

Check out the many resources on her website and sign up for her enewsletter at www.VictortiaBoyson.com.